LONG TREY NORRIS

First published in Great Britain 2003
by Egmont Books Ltd
239 Kensington High Street, London W8 6SA
Text copyright © Malachy Doyle 2003
Illustrations copyright © Sholto Walker 2003
The author and illustrator have asserted their moral rights
Paperback ISBN 1 4052 0594 6
10 9 8 7 6 5 4 3 2 1
A CIP catalogue record for this title is available from the British Library
Printed in Dubai

LONG GREY NORRIS

Malachy Doyle · Sholto Walker

YELLOW Bananas

To Kevin Crossley-Holland
with thanks for all your
support and encouragement
M.D.

For Grace, Milo and Finn
S.W.

Chapter One

BRENDAN O'DONNELL WAS out playing ball, in the five-acre field at the back of the hill, when who should he see but a long grey man, riding up on a skinny white horse.

'I'll give you a game,' said the man coming close. 'Winner Takes All!' said he. He'd a face twice as long as the head of a spade and a body the length of a boat.

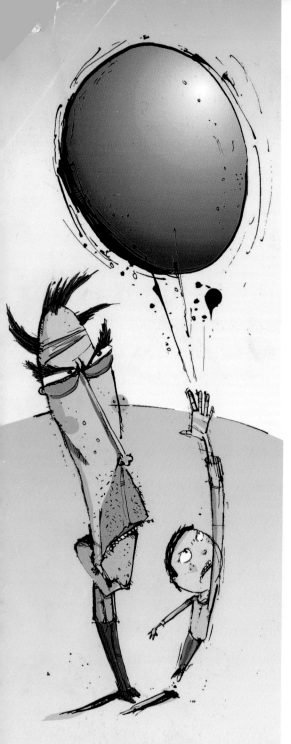

'Fair enough,' said
Brendan O'Donnell,
for he could throw
a ball higher and
catch a ball better
than anyone else
in the land. And he
tossed the ball high
in the midsummer
air and, eagle-eyed,
watched as it rose
and it fell.

A step to the left,
then a step to the
right, and he caught
it as easy as pie.

'Not bad,' said the
man, nodding, 'but
you won't be good
enough to beat me.'

'We'll soon see
about that,' said
Brendan, flinging
the ball at him.

The man caught and Brendan caught and they threw it hard and low. The man caught and Brendan caught and over and over they threw, till Brendan tossed a wonderful toss high into the sun. It dazzled the eyes of the long grey man, so the ball hit his fingers and fell to the ground with a terrible thud at his feet.

'You may have me this time, young Brendan O'Donnell,' scowled the man, ripping a brown leather bag from his waist and flinging it over, 'but I'll have you tomorrow for sure!'

'Look what I won, Gran,' called Brendan, arriving home. And he emptied a pile of shiny gold coins out on the table.

'My darling boy, we're rich!'

she cried. 'But who did it come from, this wonderful prize, and how did you manage to win it?'

'It came from a man in the five-acre field,' said Brendan, proudly. 'I beat him at throwing

and that's what I got.'

His grandmother went quiet, and a dark shadow ran across her face.

'What did he look like, this man?' she whispered.

'Ugly as sin!' said Brendan, cheerily. 'He'd a face twice as long as the head of a spade and a body the length of a boat.'

'Heaven help us, boy,' cried the old woman, holding him tightly for fear she might faint. 'That's Long Grey Norris! My own mother used to warn me of him, and her mother before. Oh, why did you let him near you, boy, for don't you know what they say?'

'What's that, Gran?'

'If you play with him once, you play to the end, and the game never stops till he wins! What did he call the game, anyway?'

'Winner Takes All,' said Brendan.

The old woman gasped. Then, without another word, she hobbled up the stairs and took to her bed, to escape from all the wickedness of the world.

Chapter Two

THE FOLLOWING DAY, Brendan was down
by the river, fishing for trout, when who should
arrive but Long Grey Norris, riding up on his
skinny white horse.

'I'll give you a race,' said the sourest of men.
'Winner Takes All, as before.'

'Fair enough,' said the boy, with a smile.
'Over the water and back.' For Brendan
O'Donnell swam further and faster than anyone
else in the land.

They threw off their clothes and they stood on the side, bending and stretching, preparing to swim.

Without a word of warning, Long Grey Norris sprang from the bank and he didn't hit water till halfway across.

Brendan swam like his back was on fire! He powered through the river as only he could, reaching the opposite bank just behind his rival. With the most skilful of turns, he slid beneath the long grey body of his opponent and surfaced ahead of him.

And with
all his remaining
strength, Brendan held
on to the lead, and
touched the riverbank,
inches ahead.

'Yes!' he cried,
punching the air in triumph.

'Huh,' said Long Grey Norris in disgust,

pondweed dripping
from his bony body
and slime dribbling
from his crooked
mouth. 'Double huh.'
And he wrenched a
black leather bag from
the saddle of his horse
and flung it over.

'You may have
me this time, young
Brendan O'Donnell,' he
snarled, 'but I'll get you
tomorrow for sure.'

13

Brendan went home and poured another pile of gold coins on to the kitchen table. 'I met him again and I beat him again, Gran,' he said, proudly. 'First it was ball and now it's at swimming. Winner Takes All, as before.'

But the words sent a chill through the heart of the woman.

'Stay clear of that man, if a man's what he is,' she told Brendan, 'or it'll all end in tears for us both.' And she took to her bed to escape from the fear that her boy would be stolen away.

Chapter Three

THIS TIME, BRENDAN tried to do as she asked, for he'd seen the fear in his poor grandmother's eyes, and he didn't want to upset her any more. He went to spend the day in the Forest of Cullin, where the trees grow deep and dark, and no one could find you in a month of slow Sundays.

He was busy gathering wood when he heard a noise behind him. Spinning round, he saw Long Grey Norris, riding up on the skinny white horse.

'Hiding, are you?' sneered the thinnest of men.

'Oh no,' said Brendan, cheerfully, 'just passing the time.'

'Well, I'll give you a race to the top of that tree,' said the man, pointing to the Great Oak, 'for it's time I got my revenge.'

Brendan nodded, despite his grandmother's warning. Sure, hadn't he climbed every tree in the county, many's the time and more? Wasn't he the champion climber in the whole of the land?

Without a
moment's delay,
Long Grey Norris
sprang from the
horse, grabbed
a high branch
and was hauling
himself up.

'That's cheating!'
cried Brendan, and
he raced to the tree.
He stretched and
he scrambled
and soon he
was nearing
him. Soon he
was equal to
Long Grey
Norris, and
soon he
was well
in the
lead.

Brendan was coming to the top of the great
tree when he saw an eagle's nest, cradled in
the only foothold, and three tiny chicks
peeping away inside. His heart leapt at the
sight, for there was nothing he loved more than
birds, and his favourite of all were the great
soaring eagles.

'I beat you at ball and I beat you at
swimming, and now it's at climbing you're
beaten, old man,' he shouted down to Long
Grey Norris. 'For there's a nest here with three
wee scaldies in it, and it wouldn't do to go on.'

'Who cares about scaldies!' cried Long Grey
Norris, climbing towards him. 'It's a race to the
top, young Brendan, and it isn't over yet!'

The boy covered the nest with his body, to protect the tiny birds, but Long Grey Norris clambered over him, raking his boots down Brendan's back as he passed.

'Hah!' called the man, at the top of the tree and the top of his voice, swinging and singing and gloating.

'Double hah!' he yelled, the words ringing out through the whole of Mayo, from the lakes to the sea, from Kinlough to Benwee.

'Triple hah!' he screamed, 'I'm the winner and the Winner Takes ALL!'

As he scrambled down, the heel of his boot  gouged Brendan again, but the boy couldn't leave the three wee scaldies to be stamped on. His back was aching from scraping and his stomach was retching from stretching, but he wasn't too sad to have lost.

Sure it's only money, he thought. We were happy enough without it, me and my gran, and we'll be happy enough again.

He led Long Grey Norris to the cottage, past the terrified old woman, and he pulled out the two leather bags from their hidey-hole.

'It's Winner Takes All, remember?' said Long Grey Norris with a sneer.

The words sent a chill through the heart of the poor woman, and she ran from the room and took to her bed, to escape from the fear that she'd lose her beloved grandson.

'I know it is,' said Brendan to Long Grey Norris. 'This is it all.'

'Oh, no,' shouted the evil man, 'it's Winner Takes ALL!'

And with a triumphant yell, he grabbed the boy by the scruff of the neck, threw him on to the back of his horse and galloped away into the dark.

Chapter Four

ALL THROUGH THE night and all through the day and into the evening they rode. Over the mountains and over the bogs and through the sad silence of woods. And at last they came to the House of Norris, where Brendan was locked in a barn.

First thing in the morning, the long grey man appeared at the door, with a face more dismal still.

'Get up out of there, young Brendan O'Donnell,' said he, 'for today I get my revenge. You're to find me a berry, as yellow as the sun, before the day's done or you're dead!'

Poor Brendan didn't much feel like dying, so he spent the whole day searching for yellow berries. He scoured the fields and the forests, the hills and the hollows, from up in the trees to down on his knees. He found blackberries, blueberries, green, white and goldberries, but never a yellow one anywhere.

As the reddening sun went down, Brendan sat on a rock with his head in his hands, hungry and heartsore, exhausted and broken.

'If only I'd listened to my gran,' he said, 'this would never have happened.'

At that moment, a hand tapped his shoulder and up he glanced, expecting to see the empty eyes of Long Grey Norris.

Instead it was a girl, with hair as dark as the sloes of October and eyes that were brighter than stars.

'I'm Orla,' she said, with a smile that lightened his sadness. 'I work in the kitchens of Long Grey Norris. Is there anything I can do?'

'I can't find a yellow berry,' said Brendan. 'And if I don't, Long Grey Norris will have my life.'

'You're not the first and you won't be the last,' said Orla, 'for he's a cruel and horrible man. Here, let me help you.'

So they searched in the brambles and crawled through the nettles, got stung and got scratched and got sore. But, try as they might, there wasn't a single yellow berry to be found.

When they heard the sound of Long Grey
Norris galloping out from his home, they ran
to a cave to hide.

'He'll find us,' said Brendan, 'and that'll be
the end of me.'

But they'd only just crawled into their hiding
place when in through the mouth of the cave
flew a golden eagle. And as it came towards
them they
saw, much
to their
delight, that
it was
carrying
a sprig
of yellow
berries in
its mouth.

'This is with thanks for saving my first scaldy, Brendan O'Donnell,' said the bird, dropping the sprig at the boy's feet.

'Oh, thank you,' said Brendan, as it flew out. 'Thank you, kind eagle.'

Brendan smiled at Orla, and they marched to the mouth of the cave, eyes downcast.

The skinny white steed of Long Grey Norris drew to a halt in front of them, and the evil horseman laughed in triumph.

'Hah!' he cried, 'I knew I'd get you this time!'

But from behind his back, Brendan drew out the sprig of yellow berries, and the expression on the face of Long Grey Norris turned from triumph to horror.

'Triple huh!' cried the man. 'You must have had help in the finding of these, for they grow in a thicket so wild and so deep, it would take you a year and a week and a day to get through!' And he spat on the ground in disgust.

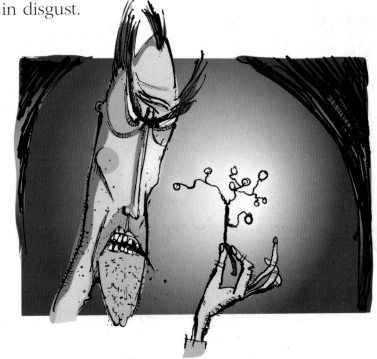

He pulled Orla and Brendan up on to his horse and galloped home, where Orla was set to making food for her master, and Brendan was locked in the barn.

He was just dropping off to sleep when the key turned in the lock and in came Orla, with a great steaming bowl of stew.

'Oh, thank you, Orla,' said Brendan, tucking into the food, for he had a terrible hunger on him.

They sat and talked into the early hours of the morning, closing their minds to the danger they were in. Orla told Brendan how she'd been tricked into service by the old man, and Brendan spoke of his home, of his grandmother, his love of the birds, and just for a while the world didn't seem such a bad place after all.

Chapter Five

AT COCKCROW THE next morning, Long Grey Norris was at the door of the barn. 'Get up out of there, young Brendan O'Donnell!' he snarled, dragging the lad out of his sleep and down to the river. 'I've another job for you, and if you don't manage it this time, you're finished. You must build me a bridge of feathers by nightfall, strong enough to walk on, or else!'

A single black feather lay on the ground next to Brendan, and a single white one on the water, but how would he find enough? And how could he make a bridge with them anyway?

He searched high and low and he gathered a few, but the wind blew, the feathers flew, and they filled the air like snowflakes. Brendan ran, trying to catch them, but it was hopeless. Every time he laid them on the riverbank, another gust of wind came and threw them into the air, so in the end he gave up, and every last one of them floated away on the breeze.

Brendan sat by the riverside, his head in his hands, as a pair of swans slid past. He looked up, saw their beautiful white coats, and had an idea. On the other side of the river, a family of ducks were swimming, overhead a flock of wild geese flew, and behind him in the wood a thousand birds were singing. There were feathers all around, he realised, if only he could bring himself to kill the birds and pluck them.

He even went so far as to cut a sapling from a willow tree and size it up for a bow, but he couldn't bring himself to make it, never mind fire it. He loved birds. How could he take the lives of so many innocent creatures just to save his own?

It was late afternoon by the time Orla found him, his head in his hands once more.

'There's no hope for me this time, Orla,' said Brendan, sadly. 'I've to build a bridge of feathers, strong enough to walk on, but it's impossible – I can't even begin.'

The girl sat down next to him and they got to talking once more.

Indeed, they were so caught up in each other that they soon forgot all about Long Grey Norris. Time slipped by and it was well into evening before Brendan at last came to his senses.

'He'll be here any minute!' he said, in a panic. 'Oh Orla, what shall I do?'

Chapter Six

AT THAT MOMENT, a golden eagle landed on the rock next to them.

'Don't fret, young Brendan,' said the eagle. 'As I told you before, we never forget those who have shown us kindness. This is with thanks for saving my second scaldy.'

The proud eagle flew to the middle of the river and suddenly the sky filled with a great swooshing as all the birds of the air and water joined the eagle on either side, spanning the river in a beautiful quivering arch.

'A bridge of feathers!' gasped Orla, as a swan glided to the bank beside her.

'Yes,' said the bird. 'And now you must cross it. Walk on my back. It won't hurt.'

Orla took Brendan by the hand and together they stepped on to the swan, all the way up the fluttering arch and down the other side, where the bird's partner waited to provide the final stepping stone.

There on the opposite bank stood Long Grey Norris, with a face as long as a wet March Monday.

'Huh!' he said, in disgust. 'Quadruple huh! You've done it again, young Brendan O'Donnell, but I'll have you tomorrow, young fellow-me-lad, I'll have you tomorrow for sure.'

And with that he turned and galloped away, so full of gloom that he forgot even to lift Brendan and Orla on to the horse behind him.

'I suppose we'd better follow him,' said
Brendan. 'What else can we do?'

'Are you mad, Brendan?' cried Orla. 'As long
as you stay, you're in danger. For you know
what they say about Long Grey Norris . . .'

'I do,' said Brendan. 'My grandmother told
me. If you play with him once, you play to the
end, and the game never stops till he wins.'

'That's right,' said Orla. 'But it's not a game
any more – it's your life, and I don't want you
to lose it. Tomorrow, he plans to send you into
the Valley of Fire, where the heat is so intense
that no one has ever come out alive.'

'What should I do?' said Brendan.

'Come with me,' said Orla. 'There's a black horse in the stable who can run like the wind. We'll ride on him together through the pitch dark night and leave this dreadful place forever.'

So they ran to the stable, she saddled up the horse and on they climbed. Orla sat up front, Brendan clung on behind, and they flew through the night. Out of the wood and over the bog, away.

When the sun was rising in the heavens, Orla cried, 'Look behind you, Brendan, and see if there's anyone there!'

Brendan glanced over his shoulder and made out a tiny figure on the horizon, a dark speck  against the orange glow of sunrise.

'It's him, Orla!' he cried. 'Go faster!'

They galloped on, raising dust as they flew, and in time the girl said, 'Look behind you again, Brendan, and tell me what you see.'

Brendan turned and saw Long Grey Norris, cracking his whip, fast approaching.

43

'He's coming, Orla!' he cried. 'Go faster!'

They raced on and they raced on, and when the sun was at its height, Orla said, 'Look again, Brendan! Where is he now?'

But before the boy even had time to turn round, he heard the beating of hooves and felt the hot breath of the demon horse on his neck.

'He's upon us, Orla!' he screamed. 'Go faster!'

'I can't!' cried Orla, for her black horse was foaming at the mouth. 'I can't!'

But out of nowhere, just in time, came the golden eagle. 'This is for saving my third scaldy!' it screeched, dropping out of the sky, until its great wings hovered between the two horses, blocking out the sun.

'Get out of my way, you stupid bird!' screamed Long Grey Norris, cracking his whip at the eagle, circling above him.

But as he did so the bird opened its beak, showering a mouthful of seeds to the ground all around him.

All in a second, up shot a thicket of spikes, so fierce and so dense that no living thing could get through. Orla's black horse was free to ride on, but the skinny white steed was trapped.

'Help!' cried Norris. 'Let me out!'

But there was no escape, forward or back, from the pressure of the spikes. All he could do was watch, first in fury and then in pain, as the dark horse sped over the hills, away.

All day they rode, Orla and Brendan, through woods, bogs and mountains until they arrived at the boy's home.

'I'm back!' he cried, as his grandmother opened the door of their cottage. 'And this is Orla, who helped me escape from Long Grey Norris.'

The old woman looked at him hard, unable to believe it could be her beloved grandson, who she had given up for dead. But when he threw his arms around her and hugged her tightly, she knew it was him.

Then she turned, and saw the girl with hair as dark as the sloes of October, with eyes that were brighter than stars, and her own filled with tears.

'A hundred thousand welcomes to you both!' she said, drawing them into the cottage. She sat them by the fire, and fetched them food and drink. But before they could even begin to tell her of their adventures she hobbled off to her bed to escape from the wonders of the world. The joy in her heart at the sight of Brendan and Orla was too much to bear, at least until morning.